Nathan Blows Out the Hanukkah Candles

To Nicole who inspired me to write this book, and to all the members of my extended family who have learned to cope with and embrace children with special needs. — T.L.W.

This book is dedicated to my son Nathan whose journey in life is an inspiration to all of us. — N.K.

This story is based on a real "Nathan," a high functioning autistic child who did blow out his family's Hanukkah candles. Autism covers a broad spectrum, and Nathan is not meant to be representative of all autistic children. Rather, this book is designed to introduce young children and families to autism and other developmental disorders. Judaism teaches acceptance of every person as a reflection of God's image, and the importance of both compassion and inclusion in the community.

Text copyright ©2011 by Tami Lehman-Wilzig with Nicole Katzman
Illustrations copyright ©2011 by Lerner Publishing Group

KAR-BEN Publishing
A division of Lerner Publishing Group, Inc.
241 First Avenue North
Minneapolis, MN 55401 U.S.A.
800-4KARBEN

Website address: www.Karben.com

Library of Congress Cataloging-in-Publication Data

Lehman-Wilzig, Tami.
    Nathan blows out the Hanukkah candles / by Tami Lehman-Wilzig ;
illustrated by Jeremy Tugeau.
        p.   cm.
    Summary: Although Jacob finds his autistic brother, Nathan, annoying, he gets angry at a new neighbor who calls Nathan weird, but their mothers help the boys get along with a special Hanukkah observance.
    ISBN 978-0-7613-6657-7 (lib. bdg. : alk. paper)
    [1. Autism—Fiction. 2. Hanukkah—Fiction. 3. Brothers—Fiction.
4. Neighborliness—Fiction. 5. Judaism—Customs and practices—Fiction.]
I. Tugeau, Jeremy, ill. II. Title.
PZ7.L53223Nat 2011
[E]—dc22   2010020278

Manufactured in the United States of America
1 - MG - 7/15/11

Nathan Blows Out the Hanukkah Candles

Tami Lehman-Wilzig
with Nicole Katzman

Illustrated by Jeremy Tugeau

KAR-BEN
PUBLISHING

"Is it Hanukkah? Is it Hanukkah?"

All my big brother does is say the same thing over and over again.

"Is it Hanukkah? Is it Hanukkah?" he keeps repeating. As usual, Nathan is lost in his own world. Then he announces, "Tonight is Hanukkah, tonight is Hanukkah."

"I know, I know," I answer.

Mom gives me a look.
"Ohh-Kay . . . Nathan's mind is wired differently."
"I'm glad you understand that, Jacob."

"Hanukkah has eight days. Hanukkah has eight days."

I think I'm going to burst.

"And the United States has fifty states," continues Nathan. "Alabama, Alaska, Arizona, Arkansas—"

Mom cuts in. "I have a good idea, Nathan. Turn on your computer and see if you can find a blank map of the United States where you can put in the state names."

Nathan goes to his room.

Mom asks me, "Would you like to help set up the Hanukkah menorah?"

"Sure," I answer. "I like pretending I'm Judah Maccabee, lighting the menorah in the Temple."

"Tonight's the first night of Hanukkah, so only one candle," Mom says. "Plus the shamash, the helper candle, for lighting it."

I'm Judah Maccabee, winning the war against King Antiochus! We recapture our holy Temple! There's a small jug of oil to light the menorah. It's enough for one day but—a miracle!—the oil lasts eight days.

Tonight I'm going to pray for a new miracle. That Nathan stops repeating himself.

I put the menorah on the table next to the window. A big truck pulls in next door, with a car behind it. A new family is moving in. Yes! It looks like there's a boy my age. I wonder if he plays basketball. "Mom!" I yell. "I'll be outside shooting hoops."

I bounce the ball really hard. It works.
My new neighbor walks over.
"Can I play?" he asks. "My name's
Steven. What's yours?"
"Jacob."

Steven and I play until Dad comes home. He has a box of fresh jelly doughnuts. "Our traditional Hanukkah dessert," he says. "Come, it's time to light the menorah."

Nathan stands right in front of the menorah. Dad uses the shamash
to light the candle. We say the blessings, then sing "Ma'oz Tzur."
Nathan stands still, staring at the lit candles.
We finish singing. Good. Now we can eat the—

"Nay-than!" I shout.
I can't believe it. I heard Nathan take a deep breath,
but I didn't think he was going to blow out the candles!
"Why did you do that?" I ask angrily.

Dad puts his arm around Nathan. "Hanukkah candles are
not like birthday candles. We don't blow them out."
"Okay," answers Nathan.
"Do you understand?" asks Mom.
I want to say "Of course not," but Nathan says, "Yes."

The next afternoon I go outside, loudly bouncing my ball again. Steven joins me, until his mother calls him to come home.

Dad's car turns in the driveway. He gets out, holding a new box of jelly doughnuts.

"Let's light the menorah!" he says.

Just as we gather, the doorbell rings.

"We're your new neighbors," says Steven's mother.
"I thought we should get to know each—"

"What's your name? What's your name?"

Nathan has rushed over and is hugging Steven. Dad quickly steps in and guides Nathan back to the menorah.

"Good," I mutter to myself. But I'm worried. I never know what Nathan will do next.

Mom hesitates, then invites the neighbors in. "Would you like to light the menorah with us?"

I try signaling no to Mom, but she ignores me.

We recite the blessings, and sing "Ma'oz Tzur." Uh-oh. Nathan's eyes are fixed on the candles. I squeeze my eyes closed. I hear Steven and his mother gasp. Yup. Nathan has blown out the candles.

"Your brother's weird," Steven whispers.

"This certainly is a different way of celebrating," says Steven's mother. "I enjoyed that."

Mom gives her a weak smile. "Why don't you kids play dreidel?"

I grab one of our wooden dreidels, motioning to Steven to sit
on the floor. We take turns spinning it. Nathan can't keep his eyes
off the whirling dreidel. Suddenly, he snatches another dreidel.

"Move away," I say, as he plops down next to me, lying on his side and propping his head up with his hand. Nathan doesn't budge. His eyes are fixed on his dreidel, which he spins, and spins, and spins—faster, and faster, and faster. On and on and on . . . and ON . . . and ON . . .

"Here we go again," I mutter.
"Let's move over there," Steven
suggests. We play until we get
hungry and we go to the dining
room for jelly doughnuts.

"Nathan!" Mom calls.
No answer. Nathan is hypnotized by his spinning dreidel.
"Nay-than!"
Still no answer.

Mom gently takes the dreidel away and brings Nathan over to the table. "Come, have a jelly doughnut with us," she says.

The next afternoon, I'm back outside, bouncing my ball. Steven
comes out, takes a deep breath, then lets out a huge puff of air.
"I'm blowing out the Hanukkah candles!" he laughs.
He repeats this every time he sees me over the next few days.

It's the seventh day of Hanukkah. I've had enough.
I go to Steven's house and ring the bell. He answers the door
and starts taking a deep breath.
"Stop making fun of my brother!" I shout. "He's autistic."
"That's the best!" Steve chuckles. "You're brother's artistic!"

"Not artistic, *autistic*. My mom says Nathan just looks at things in his own way. He thinks differently. And he helps me see the world differently."

"You're as weird as your brother," Steven says with a mean look.

The next thing I know, Steven's mother is standing next to us. "Jacob, I'm so glad to see you. Your mother invited us over tonight to celebrate the last night of Hanukkah."

"What?"

"She wants us to celebrate the way Nathan celebrates and we're happy to come, aren't we?"

Steven gulps. "Uh . . . I guess." I wonder what she means.

That evening, just before it gets dark, Steven and his parents come over. Steven's mom is carrying a large box of fresh jelly doughnuts. "We're here to help celebrate this happy holiday with you, Nathan," she says. Nathan smiles.

Our menorah is on the windowsill, with all eight candles plus the shamash in its candleholders. Dad motions all of us to come to the menorah. We light the candles, say the prayers, and sing "Ma'oz Tzur."

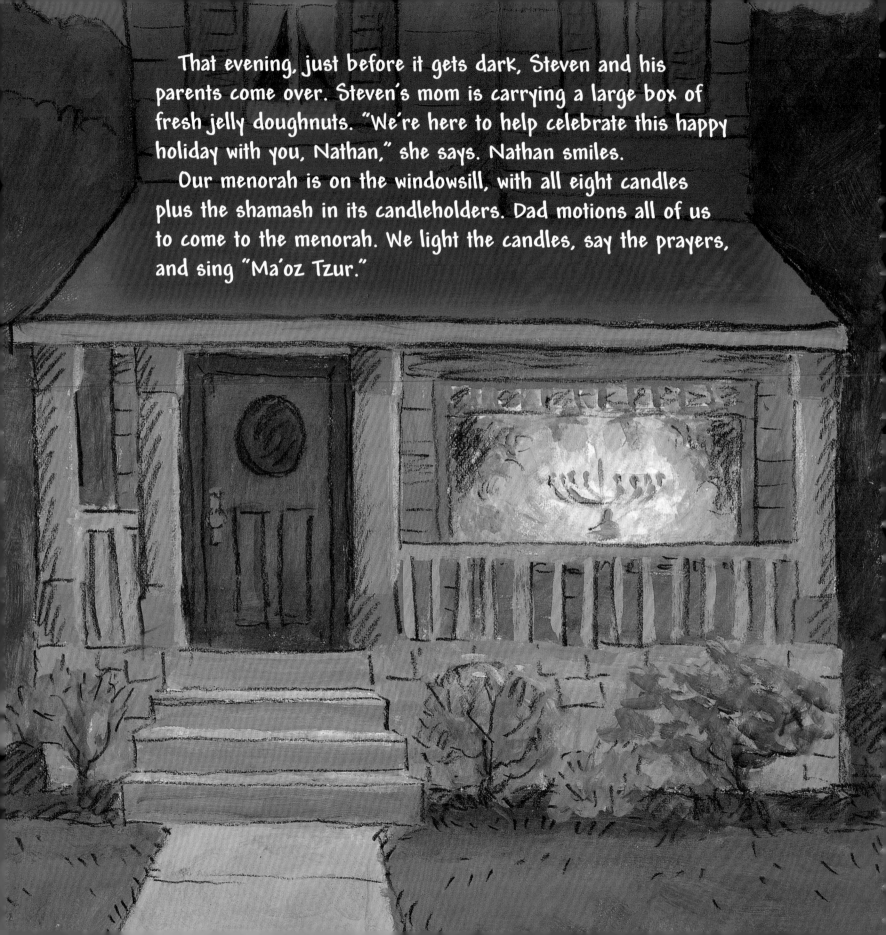

Then Mom goes to the table. She takes out nine jelly doughnuts from the box and places them in rows on a tray. She sticks a candle in the middle of each doughnut and lights them all with the shamash. Mom smiles. "Now it's time for us to celebrate Hanukkah Nathan's way."

I nudge Steven. We all go to the table where the jelly doughnuts are lined up with their candles burning brightly.
"One, two, three!" says Mom.
And we all blow! Nathan beams.

"That was awesome!" says Steven. "This is the best Hanukkah ever!"